WELCOME TO

Beast Quest

Collect the special coins in this book.
You will earn one gold coin for
every chapter you read.

Once you have finished all the chapters,
find out what to do with your gold coins at
the back of the book.

With special thanks to Allan Frewin Jones

To Freddie Mills

ORCHARD BOOKS

First published in Great Britain in 2016 by The Watts Publishing Group

1 3 5 7 9 10 8 6 4 2

Text © 2016 Beast Quest Limited.
Cover and inside illustrations by Steve Sims
© Beast Quest Limited 2016

Beast Quest is a registered trademark of Beast Quest Limited
Series created by Beast Quest Limited, London

A CIP catalogue record for this book is available from the British Library.

ISBN 978 1 40834 295 4

Printed and bound by CPI Group (UK) Ltd, Croydon, CR0 4YY

The paper and board used in this book are made from wood from responsible sources

Orchard Books
An imprint of Hachette Children's Group
Part of The Watts Publishing Group Limited
Carmelite House, 50 Victoria Embankment, London EC4Y 0DZ

An Hachette UK Company
www.hachette.co.uk
www.hachettechildrens.co.uk

DROGAN
THE JUNGLE MENACE

BY ADAM BLADE

ORCHARD

TRIAL OF HEROES

JUNGLE

CORSAIR ISLAND

CONTENTS

A great battle has just taken place in Avantia. The City was almost destroyed by a raging Beast, and many lives were at risk...

Thankfully, a courageous warrior came to our aid, and peace was restored to the capital. But this warrior was not Tom, nor was it Elenna, for they were across the ocean, fighting bravely on another Quest. Now Avantia has a new champion, laying claim to Tom's title of Master of the Beasts.

And this courageous fighter has an honest claim to that title, which means there is only one thing for it.

Tom must put his title on the line. He and his opponent must complete the Trial of Heroes.

May the bravest warrior win.

Aduro, former wizard to King Hugo

AN UNEASY ALLIANCE

Rushing water swirled around Tom as the whirlpool dragged him down.

Can't breathe! Drowning!

He tumbled through the churning water, the weight of his sword and shield pulling him deeper. Without the power of his Golden Armour he couldn't fight the deadly current.

He kicked hard, trying to push upwards, or what he thought was upwards. His chest ached painfully, as though an iron clamp were being tightened around his ribs.

Must reach the surface!

Through a flurry of bubbles, he saw Elenna's terrified face, her eyes wide with panic as she fought the savage flood.

Lights burst behind Tom's eyes. The agony in his chest was excruciating. He could feel the strength draining from his muscles. His lungs were screaming.

In moments, he would be dead.

Suddenly, the sucking sensation was gone. Gritting his teeth, he ploughed upwards, snatching at Elenna's arm and towing her along.

He saw sunbeams dancing on the surface above him. A silent cry escaped his mouth.

At last, his head burst from the water and he sucked in air. *Made it...*

He heard Elenna coughing at his side. "I thought we weren't going to escape," she said, panting.

"Me, too," Tom admitted. As he recovered, he glanced around. He'd half expected to see the ocean again, where they'd battled Soara the Stinging Spectre, but instead he found himself in the middle of a swamp. Dirty water led to mangrove forests on all sides.

The black portal had transported
them to a new destination – some
sort of humid jungle.

Tom struck out with Elenna through the choppy water towards a narrow, boggy shore, and soon his feet sank into soft mud under him. He floundered towards dry land. Elenna waded through the brown water at his side.

The air was heavy and sticky, and strange insects buzzed and flitted over the water's edge.

"You didn't drown, then," said a sarcastic voice. "I'm so very pleased about that."

Tom and Elenna clambered out of the shallows. Amelia and her uncle, Dray, were standing just under the canopy of trees. Dray was tall and bald, with greyish skin and a grim, unreadable face. Amelia was a few years older than Tom and Elenna, with long blonde hair and mocking blue eyes. It was she who had spoken. She was looking at her map, and neither of them made any attempt to help Tom and Elenna out of the clinging mud.

Tom gave Amelia a hard look, trying to swallow his anger. "We've all been lucky so far," he said. "But unless we start working together, I won't be able to protect you."

Amelia smirked. "What makes you think I need your protection?"

"Let's just stop squabbling," Elenna said, with a sigh.

"I agree," said Amelia. "We can

stop it right now if you two give up and go home." She gave Tom a superior look. "You know I'm the true Mistress of the Beasts. I'm going to complete the Trial of Heroes and claim the Golden Armour. It's inevitable – my birth right."

Tom seethed with anger and frustration, taking out his own map, which must have been made from magical parchment because it was completely dry. Amelia had shown up at King Hugo's palace in Avantia, claiming to be the direct descendant of a past Mistress of the Beasts named Kara the Fearless. Despite all the Quests that Tom had undergone, Amelia insisted that she

was the true protector of Avantia.
The former wizard, Aduro, had
consulted the ancient chronicles and
had ruled that the two candidates

had to undergo the Trial of Heroes to discover which one was worthy. It was the custom when there were competing claims.

I need to get to that axe first, Tom thought, as he scanned the map. It showed miles of jungle without end, but right in the centre flashed a red dot. Beneath it was written a name – *DROGAN.*

The next Beast...

Elenna pointed at Amelia. "You talk about going home," she said. "But where *is* your home? Where were you hiding all those years while Tom and I have been keeping Avantia and the other realms safe?"

A red flush burned across Amelia's

face. "My home is a village near the Northern Mountains," she said sharply. "My parents died when I was a child – but a wise man recognised that I was a descendent of Mistress Kara and taught me about my heritage."

Tom felt some sympathy at hearing Amelia's tale. He'd lost his father too, and had never seen his mother, Freya, when he was growing up. "We come from similar backgrounds," he said. "That's all the more reason to work together – destiny will decide who is the true Master of the Beasts."

"Mistress of the Beasts," Amelia interrupted. "And destiny needs a push every now and then." Her eyes flashed. "I deserve to win."

"You're selfish and unworthy," snapped Tom. "If not for your uncle, you would already be dead."

"And exactly who is this man you call your uncle?" exclaimed Elenna. "He was sucked into Soara's belly." Tom recalled the horrible moment clearly – they'd all thought Dray was dead. "He was underwater so long he should have drowned," Elenna continued. "How is he even alive?"

Amelia waved a dismissive hand. "My uncle is...very tough," she said.

"That's one word for it," said Elenna, eyeing Dray warily. As usual, the big brute didn't say a word.

Amelia snarled at her. "Just keep out of our way from now on, or I won't be held responsible for your fate! Come on, Uncle."

She turned and strode away under the trees. With a single, grim look at Tom and Elenna, Dray walked past her, ripping his way through the vegetation as though the leaves and ferns were no tougher than cobwebs. The jungle quickly swallowed them both.

"I don't believe a word she says," Elenna stated. "And I'm not sure that uncle of hers is even human!"

"The truth will come out eventually," said Tom. "Our first task is to complete this Quest. I wonder what sort of Beast Drogan—"

There was a frantic rustling among

the trees and, a moment later, Dray and Amelia came stumbling back into the open. Amelia's face was pale.

"What happened?" asked Tom, drawing his sword

As Amelia and Dray scrambled away from the trees, a huge scorpion scuttled into view. It was as large as a calf, its tail raised high over its back and its sting dripping yellow venom.

Is this the next Beast? Tom wondered, as the vicious creature sped forwards with pincers snapping. His pulse settled a little. *It seems quite small.* He checked the map as he backed away – no, Drogan wasn't anywhere near them.

He heard more noises from within

the jungle. Tom gasped in horror as a whole host of scorpions scurried out, each as large and dangerous as the first. They advanced, tails twitching with menace, pressing Amelia and Dray back towards the swamp.

Suddenly Tom didn't feel quite so confident.

The scorpions' pincers snapped and mouthparts clacked as they closed in from every side.

THE SCUTTLING MENACE

"Group together!" shouted Tom, as the scorpions scuttled closer. "Back to back!"

"I don't take orders from you!" Amelia cried, swinging her heavy battle-axe as she and Dray scrambled away from the hideous creatures.

Tom jabbed his sword at the

scorpions as Elenna put an arrow
to her bow and fired. The arrow
clipped a shell and shot off into
the undergrowth. Two scorpions
sprang forwards, their stings arching
over their backs. Tom swung low,
knocking one of the creatures over
in a tangle of pincers and legs; with
another swing, he severed the tail of
the other so it lay writhing on the
ground.

He could see Amelia sweeping
her unwieldy axe to and fro as the
scorpions crowded in around her.
One of the creatures snapped its
pincers on the shaft of the axe.
Amelia drew back with a scream
as the sting spat venom, which

narrowly missed her head.

To Tom's astonishment, Dray
lunged forwards, grabbing the tail
with his bare hands. The tail lashed,
the sting driving deep into Dray's
arm. The hulking man didn't even
flinch as he swung the scorpion

around then tossed it, screeching, into the swamp. He kicked another in the head, knocking it over.

Wow! He's strong!

Tom hefted his sword, driving the scorpions off, hearing arrow after arrow fly from Elenna's bow. He glanced over his shoulder. Several more scorpions were crawling away, pierced already. He struck another with the flat of his blade, the blow ringing on its thick shell.

The remaining scorpions drew back warily, then turned and scuttled into the jungle.

"Easy!" gasped Amelia, leaning on the long shaft of her axe, panting for breath.

Dray stood staring into the trees, his hand over the wound on his arm.

"Let me see that," said Elenna, looping her bow over her shoulder and striding towards him.

Tom saw Dray press the wound harder. Black blood welled through his fingers and dripped onto the ground.

Black blood? thought Tom. *Elenna might be right – maybe he isn't human.*

"I can help you," said Elenna. "I carry special herbs to treat poison."

Dray growled and took a step back.

"He'll be fine," said Amelia.

"But..." Elenna's protest was silenced as the ground beneath them trembled.

"What was that?" asked Amelia.

Tom stared into the trees. The

branches quivered as another wave of vibrations shook the jungle. "I think it may be the Beast," he said.

Amelia brought her axe up to her shoulder. "Let it come!" she said.

The four of them stood staring into the jungle. Tom strained his eyes, his every nerve stretched to breaking point as he gripped his sword and waited for the Beast to appear.

But the rumbling died away and the jungle became still again.

"It's gone," murmured Elenna.

"For the time being," added Tom. He glanced up, seeing that the sky was darkening. It would soon be night. "We should make a shelter and a fire," he said. "We can spend the night here, then go into the jungle at first light."

Amelia eyed him sourly. "Giving orders again?" she said.

"You and your uncle can do what you like," said Tom. "Elenna and I are going to make ourselves comfortable."

Amelia raised an amused eyebrow. "If you're making a fire, you'll need wood," she said. "Uncle and I will find some."

With that, she led the hulking man under the trees.

The sky was dark by the time Tom and Elenna had finished bending the supple fern leaves into a makeshift shelter and tying them together with grasses.

Elenna stared into the trees. "Amelia and Dray have been gone a long time," she said. "It wouldn't surprise me if they're hunting the Beast without us."

Tom sighed. Amelia was certainly determined. And brave. She'd shown she wasn't afraid of facing any Beast. "I've been wondering," he said. "About Epos..."

"What do you mean?" said Elenna.

"Amelia 'just happened' to appear out of nowhere to help when the flame bird went berserk," Tom said thoughtfully.

The whole Quest had begun when

Amelia had rescued Avantia from Epos, but Tom knew there was more to it than that. He'd discovered a poisoned dart under the Good Beast's wing.

"So, you don't think it was just a coincidence that the descendent of Kara turned up when she did?" said Elenna, reading his thoughts.

Tom shrugged. "I hardly know what to think," he said. He stood up, slinging his shield onto his back and drawing his sword. "I'll go and look for them."

"Be very careful in there," said his friend.

Tom pushed into the dense jungle, his eyes adjusting to the gloom as he walked stealthily under the canopy of leaves. He didn't want to shout in case he attracted the attention of more giant scorpions – or worse still, Drogan.

He hadn't gone far – maybe two hundred paces – when he heard Amelia's voice close by, speaking in a rapid, urgent mutter.

He parted the ferns, coming upon a curious scene.

Amelia was side-on to him, facing Dray, and his hand was spread on the top of her head.

"I will find the Rune of Courage fair and square," Amelia hissed.

There was a brief pause, almost as though Amelia were listening to a voice in her head.

"There's no need to resort to that!" she mumbled. "Tom's only a boy!"

Tom stared into Dray's face. The grey man's eyes were closed, as though he

was in some sort of trance. He didn't speak.

Amelia's face suddenly twisted in pain and she dropped to her knees, her hands at her temples. "Yes!" she cried, still as if replying to a voice Tom couldn't hear. "I'm loyal to you! You know I am!"

Tom pushed through the ferns, instinctively running to her aid. He shoved Dray aside, reaching down to help Amelia to her feet.

She glared at him, batting his hand aside as she got up.

"What are you doing here?" she exclaimed. "Spying on us?"

"I came to see if you were all right," said Tom, surprised by her sudden flare of anger.

"I'm fine," Amelia snapped. "Come on, Uncle, let's get out of here."

Dray picked up a huge bundle of firewood and began to walk away.

"What's going on?" asked Tom.

"Mind your own business," said Amelia. She strode out of the clearing after Dray.

Tom followed, his mind filled with the image of the pain and alarm on Amelia's face as she had been driven to her knees.

Who had she been talking to? And what hold did the secret voice have over her?

THE BEAST IN THE TREES

Tom was awoken by the ground rocking under him. He sat up, instantly alert.

Thooom!

The ground vibrated again.

Thooom!

He peered from the shelter. Silvery early morning light filled the sky. The jungle air was misty and damp.

The fire had burned low during the night. Elenna lay close by, but the makeshift beds of leaves where Amelia and Dray had slept were empty.

"Elenna!" He shook her awake, then grabbed his sword and shield and stepped out of the shelter.

Elenna sat up, rubbing her eyes. "How long have they been gone?" she asked.

"I don't know."

Thooom!

"Do you think it's the Beast?"

Tom quickly checked the map. Sure enough, the red dot was moving. He nodded, wondering again what kind of Beast could shake the earth like that.

He spotted two sets of footprints heading into the jungle. "We have to follow Amelia and Dray. You take the lead – you're better at tracking."

Elenna snatched up her quiver and bow, then traced the line of prints into the jungle with Tom right behind her.

Tom guessed their companions had headed off before dawn in the hope of defeating the Beast alone. Amelia would do anything to prove herself Mistress of the Beasts.

"Broken branches," Elenna murmured, pointing at a recently split limb around head height.

Tom saw deep gouges in the bark of a nearby tree. They looked like the sort of marks a bear would make, but the spacing between them was wrong. *No bear could be that big.* He crept towards it, running his fingers over the marks. Then he

spotted a tuft of rough golden fur at the base. There were more clumps of hair higher among the branches.

"He definitely came through here," said Elenna. "But what kind of creature moves up in the trees and along the ground as well?" She stopped suddenly, staring down at something on the ground.

"What is it?" said Tom.

Elenna knelt and began to drag tangled ferns out of the way.

"It's a shield," she said, lifting it from the undergrowth. Tom saw it was circular, crumpled and spotted with rust, as though it had lain there for a very long time. Elenna handed it to him, and brushed some mud off to reveal four distinct dents, smashing into the shield like the knuckle-prints of an immense fist.

Tom swallowed as he saw the dim

outline of a coat of arms. *A triple-headed dog.* He looked at Elenna. "I've seen this emblem before... in the Chronicles of Avantia. It's the emblem of a noble family. They were Masters of the Beasts over two hundred years ago."

"Their shield has been lying here for all that time?" breathed Elenna.

"Remember what Daltec said," Tom murmured. "We're not the first to undertake the Trial of Heroes. I guess this poor warrior didn't survive to the end."

He set the shield down again, saddened to think of its ancient owner – and reminded starkly that for some, the Trial of Heroes led only to death. *That won't happen this time,* he vowed.

"Which way now?" he asked Elenna.

She was about to reply, when the ground under them trembled once more. Leaves rained down and the branches rustled so that it sounded as though the jungle were whispering in fear.

Thoom! Thoom! Thoom!

Something was powering towards them with a thunderous stride. Tom didn't need the map to know they were about to encounter the next Beast.

Elenna quickly put an arrow to her string as Tom slid his shield off his back and drew his sword.

THOOM!

From high above them came the sound of something ripping at the trees. Tom stared up. The canopy of leaves was shuddering.

Suddenly, the branches were wrenched aside and the great, wrinkled face of a huge ape stared down at them ferociously.

Its eyes blazed with fury under a heavy brow and its mouth was stretched in a deadly leer that revealed rows of dagger-shaped yellow fangs. Its nostrils flared in an angry snort. Even from that height, Tom reeled from the fearsome stench of its breath.

"What *is* that?" cried Elenna,
aiming her arrow into the trees.

The Beast's jaws gaped and it let
out a terrifying roar.

"It's Drogan!" Tom shouted.

And with the terrible roar still echoing in Tom's ears, the Beast dropped through the air, huge clawed hands reaching out to tear them to pieces.

4

CRUSHING FISTS

Tom pushed Elenna to one side and
flung himself to the other as the
Beast plummeted down through
the branches. It crashed into the
ground where they'd been standing a
moment before.

Tom stumbled to his feet, taking
cover behind a spray of ferns.

Drogan was crouched on his

haunches. The Beast was shaped like a gigantic gorilla, covered with dense, wiry, dirty gold fur. Its brawny arms looked like they could crush the life out of an ox. His head jerked back and forth, his wide nostrils flaring as he sniffed for his prey. With a roar, he began to pummel the earth with his huge fists, shaking the jungle to its roots.

Tom shrank back as the Beast went into a frenzy, ripping up ferns and throwing them wildly about, flinging himself into the trees, wrenching them up by the roots and hurling huge trunks through the air.

If he finds us, we're finished.

Tom glimpsed Elenna through the

undergrowth. She had picked up the
battered, dented old shield and slung
it over her shoulder. She had an arrow
drawn on her bowstring and was
shifting about for a good line of shot.

Drogan paused, his foul breath coming in stinking snorts. Then he turned his head in Elenna's direction. His eyes burned as he bared his fangs in a grimace.

He's heard her... I need to distract him somehow.

Tom fished for a branch on the ground and threw it as hard as he could from his hiding place. It rattled the limbs of a tree opposite, and the Beast spun round to face the new noise. Tom ducked away at once and sprinted back to where Elenna stood.

Drogan began shouldering through the vegetation in the other direction, growling madly and thumping his broad chest.

Tom had almost reached Elenna
when she loosed an arrow.

It was a perfect shot, striking the
Beast's shoulder. But the fur was so
thick, the arrow just bounced off.

Drogan turned slowly and looked
at the shaft on the ground. Then he
launched himself with a terrifying
speed towards where they crouched.

Tom and Elenna turned to run,
but the Beast's stamping feet shook
the ground so hard that Tom lost
his footing and stumbled forwards,
falling flat on his face.

Elenna skidded to a halt and
turned around, reaching down...

Fear tightened across Tom's chest
as Drogan loomed over them, the

air thick with his stink. The ape
smashed down his fist.

Tom pulled Elenna aside, flinging
up his shield at the same time. The
blow lifted him off his feet and sent
him spinning through the trees. He

crashed into the ground and pain shot
across his shoulder. Before he could
catch his breath or work out what
had happened to Elenna, he saw the
Beast's leathery foot stamping down.
Tom rolled out of the way as the bone-

crunching heel struck the jungle floor where his head had been. Clods of earth exploded outwards.

Through the dust, Tom saw the Beast's mighty chest rising and falling. Drogan lifted a foot and looked beneath, as if expecting to see Tom's crushed corpse. When he didn't he snarled and raised both hands, beating the ground.

"Tom?" called Elenna.

She staggered into view, bleeding from a cut to her temple and looking dazed. She saw the Beast and froze. Too late. The Beast's glinting eyes locked on to her.

"No...!" Tom cried. Gathering all his remaining strength, he stumbled to his feet and leaped onto the Beast's back. He clung to Drogan's fur as he lumbered through the trees towards Elenna. She turned and ran.

If I can land one good blow, I may be able to bring him down, Tom thought. Gritting his teeth, he began to clamber up the wiry orange fur. He wasn't sure he had the power to fell Drogan, but he had no other plan, and the Beast was closing on Elenna with fearsome speed.

Ahead, his injured friend tripped on a root and sprawled headlong. Her bow jolted out of her hand.

As Drogan leapt into the air, Tom gripped his shield with both hands

and swung it with all his might at
the Beast's ear.

Drogan howled in pain, stumbling
onto one knee. His vicious claws
swiped, but Tom was too quick –
he leapt over the scything claw
and flung himself into the trees.

Catching hold of a thin branch, he swung down and let go, dropping feet first through the ferns.

The dazed Beast stumbled clumsily into a tree, clutching his ear, while Tom rushed to Elenna's side. Helping her up, he pushed her bow into her hands. Then he ran, dragging his friend along with him.

"I thought the Beast had killed you," Elenna said, gasping.

"He nearly did." Tom panted as they raced through the ferns. He glanced over his shoulder. "We need a plan. It won't be long until..."

Drogan came bounding along the forest floor on all fours, hind legs propelling him with incredible speed and knuckles smashing into the ground with every leaping step.

We can't outrun him, Tom thought desperately.

"This way!" Amelia's urgent voice rang from his left.

Tom darted aside, tugging Elenna with him. Drogan swerved to follow them, roaring and smashing everything in his path.

Tom noticed Dray crouching in the branches of a tree above them, about twenty paces away. Huge as Amelia's uncle was, surely he didn't think that he could ambush Drogan and defeat the Beast by strength alone?

Tom flicked a look over his shoulder. Drogan was eating up the ground, swinging his arms to snatch at them. Tom put on a spurt of speed, but a root snagged his foot and he fell heavily, the wind knocked out of him. He heard Elenna yell, but before he could recover, a massive fist closed around his ankle and he felt himself hoisted upside-down into the air.

Drogan shook him, jarring the sword and shield from his grip. Tom watched helplessly as they fell to the jungle floor, out of reach. The fingers tightened around Tom's leg, claws digging into his flesh, and the Beast lifted him higher, level with his ugly, wrinkled face. Drogan's hate-filled eyes blazed and his jaws stretched wide. Thick saliva sprayed from the red throat into Tom's face as the Beast roared. Tom tried to kick out, but Drogan's grip was too strong. Terror flooded through him.

Tom heard the whizz of arrows as Elenna fired at the Beast. Some of the arrows tangled in the wiry fur, but others pierced Drogan's arm.

It's as if he doesn't even feel them.

Tom, blood rushing to his head, saw Dray still squatting high in the branches, watching expressionlessly. He was doing nothing to help.

Where's Amelia? Is she hoping I'll be killed so she that can claim the title of Mistress of the Beasts?

Then Drogan began to move Tom towards his mouth, towards his

chomping yellow teeth. Tom flailed
helpless against the vice-like grip.

He's going to eat me alive!

5

AMELIA TRIUMPHANT

Tom saw a dark shape swinging through the air. It struck Drogan on the side of the head like a giant hammer, sending the Beast staggering sideways, his face twisted in pain, his eyes rolling. A deep groan escaped his thick lips.

The forest flashed past as Drogan

slammed into the ground and Tom thumped down too, still clutched in the Beast's fist. The leathery palm cushioned his fall, but still knocked the breath from his lungs. Looking up, he saw a log swinging on vines. *So that's what knocked him out!*

Tom struggled to get loose, but the fallen Beast's fingers were still locked around him. *I wish I had the Golden Armour right now,* Tom thought. As he tried to fight his way free, Elenna came bounding through the ferns, fear etched on her face.

"You're alive! Thank goodness!" She snatched hold of Drogan's thumb with both hands and heaving back with all her strength.

Tom helped push the thumb open and at last he was able to wriggle free. He stood facing Elenna, hurting all over.

At least I'm still breathing.

"Thank you," he croaked, massaging his ribs. "That was too close."

Elenna put her hand over her mouth as she stared at the immense form of the fallen gorilla, sprawled out across the ground. There was pity in her eyes. "Is he…dead?"

Drogan was completely still, his
huge chest not moving at all.

Tom took a step towards the
Beast's head.

Amelia stepped out of the
undergrowth. "I hope he's dead," she
said, leaping up onto Drogan's chest.
She raised her arms in triumph,

spreading her feet like a victorious warrior. She sniffed, grimacing in disgust. "Ew!" She wafted a hand in front of her nose. "It smells like rotting meat!"

Tom frowned at her. "You shouldn't be glad that such a magnificent Beast is dead," he said. "A Master should first try to protect all Beasts."

Amelia stood with her fists on her hips. "I saved your life," she said. "A polite person might say 'Thanks'." She pointed up to the log, still swinging from among the high branches. "Dray did the heavy lifting for me," she added smugly. "But the trap was my idea." She looked down at Tom. "And what was your idea? Oh, yes, I remember – to get chomped. How do you think that would have ended if not for me and my uncle?"

Tom forced himself to stay calm. "Thank you for saving me," he said.

Elenna glowered up at Amelia. "And that's more thanks than we ever got for all the times we've saved you," she said, as she stooped to pick up her fallen arrows.

Amelia ignored her, gazing around with a frown. "Where's the next portal?" she asked. "Isn't it supposed to appear as soon as a Beast is vanquished?"

Tom peered about too, as he

retrieved his own weapons. *She's right. Normally the magic of the trial would be sending us somewhere new.*

Elenna nudged him. She still had the battered old shield on her shoulder.

"I found something," she told Tom, drawing him to one side so tall ferns shielded them from Amelia, who was still stomping around searching for the portal.

Elenna took the shield off her shoulder and showed Tom a small metal flap that opened to reveal a hidden chamber. A spool of thread was wound up inside.

"What do you think it's for?"

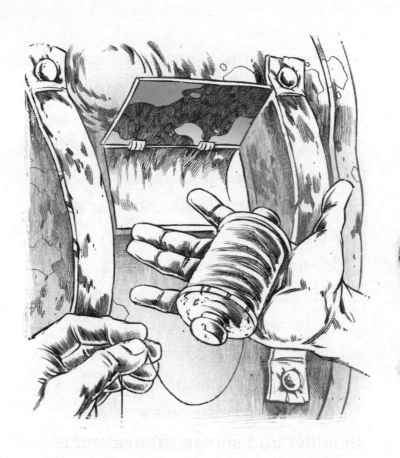

Elenna asked softly, drawing it out
and tugging it between her fingers.
"It's very strong – it might even be
magical."

"I don't know," Tom said, puzzled. "Put it somewhere safe. It could come in useful." He turned, hoping Amelia hadn't seen the thread. She was quite capable of stealing it if she thought it would help her win the trial.

But a movement a little way away caught his attention and made him draw in his breath sharply.

Drogan's fingers were twitching.

"Get away from the Beast," Tom shouted to Amelia. "Now!"

"Why? So you can take my place and pretend you defeated him?" Amelia called down. She gave a thick arm a kick. "Stupid dead monkey!"

"He's not a monkey, he's an ape," cried Elenna.

"And he's not dead!" shouted Tom, as the Beast's arm flexed.

Amelia staggered. "He's breathing!" she squealed, as the huge chest heaved.

Tom could hear the air rasping in the Beast's throat.

He's not awake yet. Perhaps there's still time to—

Drogan's eyes flicked open.

THE ROARING TERROR

The Beast sat up, roaring in fury, his fists pounding down on the ground like two mighty hammers.

The giant gorilla turned towards Amelia, snatching at her as she leaped back and ducked behind Dray. Her uncle stood firm, his arms folded, face emotionless as he gazed up into Drogan's eyes.

"We're not your enemies," Amelia cried from the cover of Dray's broad back. "There's no need for you to eat us."

Drogan got to his feet, snorting and snarling.

"Trust me," shouted Amelia in a panic. "We're not your enemies."

A movement in the high branches caught the Beast's attention. He stared up to the swinging log in its cradle of vines. Grunting angrily, he raised one arm and plucked the log down, ripping it free of the vines and taking it in both hands like a gigantic club.

"No, no, no," squealed Amelia,

pointing over Drogan's shoulder at Tom and Elenna. "The trap was their idea."

What a coward! thought Tom. *Even by her standards!*

Drogan let out a roar and swung the log in a great circle. Tom and Elenna flung themselves to the ground as it whistled above them.

Amelia screamed as Drogan turned and swung the huge club at her and Dray. Amelia threw herself to the ground, but Dray stood in its path, his feet planted resolutely.

The club ripped him off his feet, sending him crashing backwards through the trees. Tom winced at the sickening thud of the log hitting the

man's flesh. No human could hope to
survive a blow like that.

Amelia stood frozen to the spot,
her hand to her mouth, her eyes wide
with terror. "No!"

Drogan raised the club again. He lurched forwards, towering over Amelia, the club poised to deliver a killing blow. Whether it was the shock of her uncle's death, or simply fear of the Beast, the girl was as still as a statue.

Tom rushed forwards, grabbed Amelia around the waist and dived into the ferns as the club smashed down, only just missing them.

The whole world seemed to shake, trees creaking as they swayed, broken branches raining down as Tom crouched protectively over the sprawling Amelia.

"Stay here!" Tom hissed in Amelia's ear. He jumped up, brandished his

sword and beat it against his shield
to attract the Beast's attention as he
led the creature away from Amelia.

"Drogan!" he cried. "Let's settle
this!"

The Beast's drooling lips drew
back over his hideous teeth. Tom
noticed a massive old tree and ran
to stand beside it, a plan forming in
his mind.

Drogan heaved the club in a low
arc. Tom tensed his muscles, wishing
he still had the leaping power of his
golden boots. He gritted his teeth,
waiting for the perfect moment.

*If I get this wrong, I'll be dead
like Dray.*

He bounded high, tucking his legs

under him as the club whirled past.
There was a deafening crash as the
club struck the trunk of the tree.
Drogan let out a howl as the shock of
the impact forced the club from his

claws. Drogan's eyes fixed on Tom, brimming with hatred and menace. He lunged, ragged nails reaching to grab Tom.

Tom leaped forwards, lifting his sword high. He vaulted the groping fingers, stabbing down sharply.

Drogan howled as the point of the blade pricked the flesh of his hand.

Tom skidded behind a huge tree, catching his breath, his ears filled with the bellowing of the Beast. Drogan rounded on him, swiping again, but Tom ducked and rolled, aiming a quick stab at the Beast's hand before springing to his feet.

With Drogan's howls rattling his eardrums, Tom took his chance and ran; but almost at once heard the tearing and shredding sounds of the Beast in pursuit.

In a straight line, he'll always win – but I'm more agile.

Tom waited until he felt the Beast's breath hot on the back of his neck before he skidded to a halt, spinning on his toes and diving between the Beast's legs. He tucked himself into a tight ball, rolling once, twice...

Drogan shambled to a halt, twisting around.

Tom was on his feet again, but the Beast reacted more quickly than he had hoped. With a swipe of one hand, Drogan knocked Tom's sword out of his grip.

Tom lifted his shield, but the backswing of the Beast's hand smashed him to the ground. Dazed, he struggled to get to his feet, but Drogan's fingers closed around his waist and the howling Beast flung him high into the air like a rag doll.

7

THE TANGLED THREAD

The sky wheeled around Tom as he hurtled through the air above the trees, his arms and legs flailing. Then he thumped into a branch. His vision was a blur as he tumbled down through the upper reaches of the tree, jolting from one limb to the next. At last he managed to grab

one and hold on, gasping for breath.
His body felt like one throbbing
bruise.

He scrabbled around with his
feet, finding a secure branch to take

his weight. He could hear Drogan stomping down below.

Tom lowered himself carefully through the branches. He could see Drogan, the Beast's huge back bent, the long arms scrabbling through the undergrowth.

He's searching for me. Looking to finish me off.

Tom imagined what would have happened if he had fallen to the ground. Those great feet or pounding fists would have crushed him to death in an instant. But now he had a few precious moments to try and think of a way to defeat Drogan.

Snorting, the mighty ape reared

up on his haunches and beat his chest. Then Drogan seemed to hear something through the trees. The Beast paused, head tilted, listening, fingers clenching and unclenching.

With a roar that almost startled Tom into falling from his perch, Drogan stormed off through the jungle.

Tom felt his gut churn with dread. *Has the Beast heard Elenna?*

He quickly dropped down to the ground and ran as fast as he could after Drogan, limping on a numb leg, his ribs aching. The trail was easy to follow – a wide swathe of destruction through the jungle, tufts of golden hair on broken branches.

Then he heard a soft murmuring off to one side. He paused, listening intently.

"Hush!"

It was Elenna's voice. Urgent and anxious.

"The Beast can't hear us, stop whining!" That was Amelia.

"We have to go back and find Tom," Elenna whispered.

"Tom is dead," said Amelia. "I saw it with my own eyes. Drogan threw him high into the air."

"No!" said Elenna.

"Yes! Which means I'm now Mistress of the Beasts, whether you like it or not, so you need to start doing what I tell you."

"That will never happen!" Elenna said fiercely. "And I won't believe Tom is dead until I see his body!"

"Please yourself," spat Amelia. "But it's not going to be a pleasant sight. Blood and bones and guts all over, I expect!"

"Shut up!" Elenna's voice grew louder and suddenly she appeared out of the undergrowth right in front of Tom. Her face exploded into a huge smile. "I knew you weren't dead!" she exclaimed. "I have this for you." She held out Tom's sword.

Tom took it, eyeing Amelia grimly as she strode up to them.

"He looks well for a corpse, doesn't he?" Elenna said to her.

"You've more lives than a Gorgonian wildcat," Amelia said coldly. Her eyes narrowed. "But staying alive is different from actually standing up and defeating the Beast. I think you should challenge Drogan to a test of strength – face to face. That would be an honourable thing for a hopeful little hero to do."

Tom ignored her jibes. "We can't win by strength alone," he said. "We need to outsmart this Beast."

Amelia's eyebrow arched. "And are you clever enough to outsmart a monkey?" she asked.

"An ape!" Elenna broke in. "How many more times?"

"I have an idea," said Tom, as his eyes fell on Elenna's battered shield. As he spoke, the jungle reverberated to the distant thumping of the Beast's steps, and the trees shook with an angry roar. "We need to draw him back here," Tom continued. "I can do that, but you need to play your part. Elenna, that thread you found in the old shield – you and Amelia should unwind it and string it between those two trunks over there." He pointed to a pair of sturdy trees. "I'll get Drogan to chase me and when he trips over the cord, I'll put my sword to his throat and force him to surrender!"

Amelia gave a scoffing laugh. "Good luck with that," she sneered. "And what if Drogan grabs you and tears your head off, instead of giving up?"

"That won't happen if we work together," said Tom.

"I don't take orders from you," Amelia snapped.

"Listen to me," Tom said. "This isn't about proving which of us is more worthy. This is about surviving." He looked hard into her eyes. "Drogan has already killed your uncle – and who knows how many others who took the trial over the years. We have to stop him."

Amelia just shrugged. "It's a stupid plan, but I'll go along with it," she said. Tom wondered if she really cared about Dray at all. He watched as she pushed through the ferns, looking back at Elenna. "Are you coming or what?"

Elenna gave Tom an exasperated

look, then shook her head resignedly and followed, unspooling the fine thread as she did so.

"Good luck," Tom called after them. He only hoped the cord would hold.

"You too," Elenna called back.

Gripping his sword, Tom ran ahead, pursuing the unmistakable sounds of the rampaging Beast. He found Drogan stamping in a clearing. Elenna and Amelia would have had plenty of time to get the cord in place.

Tom put his fingers to his lips and let out a shrill whistle. Drogan started, his head turning sharply at the sound. Whistling again, Tom backed off. Drogan spun around, eyes peering through the trees.

"Drogan!" Tom shouted, grabbing a branch and shaking it to attract the giant ape's attention. Drogan's eyes filled with an evil light. He lurched forwards, roaring.

Tom turned and ran, leaping roots, ducking under low braches, ferns whipping his face as he sprinted through the jungle.

With Drogan in hot pursuit, he saw the two trees just ahead. There was the trip wire, just as he had planned. He gathered his strength and leaped over it. He could see Amelia and Elenna peering out from behind one of the trees.

The plan was working. Drogan was almost on top of him.

Any moment now!

His heart sank to his boots as the Beast bounded over the tripwire and came hammering down right in front of him, sending shockwaves through the ground. Drogan had avoided the trap! The gorilla-Beast set its eyes on Tom.

Tom sprang up, grabbing a branch and pulling himself higher into a vine-laden tree, his swinging legs giving him the momentum he needed to vault up to the next branch. He continued to climb, fear driving his strength. The forest floor meant certain death.

Through the hanging vines, he saw Drogan snarl in a sinister smile. He caught the trunk of the tree between both hands and shook it wildly. Tom clung on as best he could as the tree buckled and bent under him.

Crack!

The trunk broke into jagged
splinters at the base and Tom's
stomach flipped as it began to
topple. He hurled himself out of the
branches, swinging on a vine and
landing on Drogan's back. As the
tree sagged and fell, Tom managed
to loop the jungle tendril around the
ape's thick neck. Digging his heels in,
he hauled on the vine, tightening it
around Dragon's throat.

The Beast staggered to and fro,
clawing at the vine. From his lips
came great choking coughs as Tom
heaved back with every ounce of his
strength. The vine dug deep into the
orange fur, but would it be enough?

Tom saw Elenna run out from cover, one end of the thread in her hands. She raced through Drogan's legs, winding the thread around the Beast's ankles, diving in and out to make an unescapable knot.

Tom gave a last mighty tug on the vine. The Beast wheezed, losing balance, unable to shift his tangled feet. Elenna dived aside as Drogan toppled over, right towards the jagged broken tree stump.

There was a sickening thump as the Beast hit the ground chest first. Tom was flung headlong from Drogan's shoulders, and the vine tore through his grip.

He landed in a roll, leaping up,

his sword ready. Elenna had an arrow pointed at Drogan's head, and Amelia brandished her axe.

But the fallen Beast made no move. A pitiful gasp escaped his lips, and his eyes drifted closed.

Tom realised the stump must have impaled Drogan.

The jungle menace was dead.

8

BACK FROM THE DEAD

Tom bowed his head sadly. *I did not become Master of the Beasts to kill,* he thought.

Elenna came up to his side, her face solemn.

"At least he didn't suffer," she said quietly.

Tom nodded. "Thank you," he said.

"Without your quick thinking,
I would have been killed."

"We're a team," Elenna said.

"You were lucky," said Amelia,
giving the Beast a poke with her
battle-axe.

Tom glanced at her. Despite her casual comments, he could tell she was relieved that the battle was over.

"I'm sorry that Dray died," he said. "I'd be happy to help you find his body, if you'd like to give him a proper burial."

Amelia shrugged. "There's no point," she said.

Tom gave her a puzzled look. How could she be so indifferent to her uncle's death?

Before he had time to speak, he saw Drogan's body begin to fade away. In a few moments, the Beast was gone, leaving only the broken stump and crushed foliage to show

where he had fallen. Tom knew from
the other Quests that Drogan was
not gone for ever. The magic of the
Trial of Heroes would bring him
back, when another claimant to the
title dared to venture this way.

"I still don't see the portal,"
Elenna said, gazing around.
"Perhaps we need to search?"

"Do you feel that?" asked Amelia.
A slight vibration rippled through
the ground, making the ferns and

branches tremble. She swallowed. "Another Beast?"

"I don't think so," said Tom, seeing a black crack opening up where Drogan's body had been. The split widened like a yawning mouth and the quivering in the ground stopped. The jungle was strangely silent, the air thick and heavy as Tom stepped cautiously towards the gaping hole and peered in.

The blackness plunged down to impossible depths.

"Do you think that's our route?" said Elenna, standing at the very edge of the darkness.

"I don't know," said Tom.

"Let's see, shall we?" said Amelia.

She stepped up behind Elenna and shoved her over the edge.

Elenna teetered on the lip of the hole for a moment, arms wheeling

for balance, then plunged over the side with a cry of terror.

"No!" Tom reached for her a moment too late and watched Elenna's body disappear into the blackness. Her scream faded quickly. He turned on Amelia, gripping his sword, its point at her throat. "I'll make you pay for that!" he snarled.

Amelia looked coolly at him. "Calm down, little hero," she said. "I didn't hear a thud so it must be safe." She took a step forward and jumped into the portal. The last thing Tom saw was her grinning face looking up at him.

She had risked Elenna's life

to make sure the portal wasn't dangerous. Tom was tired of Amelia's selfish games. But there was no time to think about that now. He had to follow to make sure Amelia didn't do anything else to harm Elenna when they reached the other side.

He readied himself to leap into the portal when a heavy hand came down on his shoulder, jerking him back. He spun around and found himself staring up into the calm face of Amelia's uncle, Dray.

"You!" he said. "That's not possible. I saw you—"

A fist thumped into Tom's stomach. He doubled over, pitching forward onto the ground, all the breath beaten out of him.

Dray loomed over him, snatching Tom's arm and twisting it behind his back. Tom cried out in agony.

Dray's other huge hand came smacking down on Tom's head, gripping his skull so that he was unable to move.

"Who are you?" Tom wheezed, fighting for breath through the pain.

A familiar voice echoed in his mind.

"Dray is my friend – my vessel, if you prefer."

"Jezrin!"

The fingers tightened across Tom's temples, threatening to crush his skull.

"Correct, Tom. Dray has been guarding Amelia and making sure she obeys my wishes. He's a powerful creature, is he not?" Cruel laughter pierced Tom's mind and he felt all his strength bleeding away. "Give up the Quest, boy – you can't possibly win."

The truth hit Tom like a thunderbolt. "The dart! You poisoned Epos to make her evil!" His mind was swimming. "You brought Amelia to the City to claim the Golden Armour. It was you all along!"

His shoulder was close to breaking as Dray pushed the twisted arm higher still. "Has it really taken you this long to work that out?" mocked the Evil Wizard's voice.

"While there's blood in my veins,

I'll fight you," Tom said, gasping. "I'll complete the Trial of Heroes and prove myself worthy to be Master of the Beasts." He took a shaky breath. "I will never allow you and Amelia to take that from me!"

The ground shook and Tom saw that the portal was beginning to close again.

"The final stage of the trial is closed to you," snarled Jezrin. "Amelia will kill Elenna and win the Golden Armour." There was more laughter. "And you will be lost in this jungle for the rest of your pitiful life!" The laughter welled up, filling Tom's mind.

Tom gathered what little strength he had left, blotting out Jezrin's taunting voice as he steeled himself for one last, desperate effort.

He pushed off the ground with his free hand, muscles shrieking in pain as he brought the back of his head up hard into Dray's face. The big man staggered back. Tom jumped after him, driving a foot into his enemy's gut. His heel met rock-hard muscle. Dray caught his leg and threw him sideways.

Tom stood up, his arm hanging almost uselessly at his side.

Behind Dray the portal had almost vanished. There was no way past.

The grey-skinned brute smiled,

and Tom knew it was Jezrin staring through the pale eyes.

He thinks he's won. He thinks I'm trapped here. Well, he's wrong. This Quest is not over.

Tom summoned a deep breath and charged straight at his enemy. Dray lifted his fists, but Tom dived into his midriff with all the force he could muster.

His momentum was enough.
Dray wheezed and staggered back. Together, the two of them tumbled into the abyss.

Everything went black.

THE END

CONGRATULATIONS, YOU HAVE COMPLETED THIS QUEST!

At the end of each chapter you were awarded a special gold coin.
The QUEST in this book was worth an amazing 8 coins.

Look at the Beast Quest totem picture inside the back cover of this book to see how far you've come in your journey to become

MASTER OF THE BEASTS.

The more books you read, the more coins you will collect!

Do you want your own
Beast Quest Totem?
1. Cut out and collect the coin below
2. Go to the Beast Quest website
3. Download and print out your totem
4. Add your coin to the totem
www.beastquest.co.uk/totem

Don't miss the next exciting Beast Quest book, KARIXA THE DIAMOND WARRIOR!

Read on for a sneak peek...

CRASH LANDING

Tom plummeted through empty space, his fist clamped tight about Dray's tunic collar. His head throbbed from where he'd head-butted the brute before dragging them both into the abyss. Tom blinked hard, forcing Dray's broad face into focus. Dark eyes glared back at him from above a crooked broken nose. Dray let out a growl, baring his tombstone teeth in a snarl of animal rage.

Fierce anger boiled inside Tom. How could Amelia be so devious? She'd told Tom Dray was her uncle, when in fact he was a monster, created by the Evil Wizard, Jezrin.

Still groggy, Tom lifted his sword. He brought it down, hilt-first, towards the imposter's skull. Dray thrust his powerful wrists upwards and out, blocking the blow, tearing free of Tom's grip and smashing the sword from his fingers. With a stab of alarm, Tom watched his weapon spin away. He couldn't let Dray escape. He groped for the big man's shoulder, just missing. Dray swung his fist.

"Oof!" The blow landed square in Tom's chest, punching the air from his lungs and sending him

tumbling head over heels through the darkness.

Tom's stomach lurched as he spun. He stared into the blackness, looking for Dray, but couldn't see a thing. He struggled, pumping his arms and legs, trying to right himself, but the air gave no resistance, and he didn't even know which way was up any more.

Then a faint light appeared, spiralling towards him at terrifying speed – a pale gash, getting bigger and brighter by the moment.

The next portal, Tom realised. *The final stage of the Trial of Heroes!* Through the jagged rip, he saw a steep, rocky slope scattered with rubble. A shock of adrenaline jolted him. *I'm going way too fast!* Tom twisted, somehow managing to angle his feet towards the portal. He braced himself…

This is going to hurt. A lot.

He landed with a thud, feet-first on loose scree. His ankle buckled, and he tipped forwards, pitching headfirst down the slope…

"Urgh!" Tom skidded on his belly, sharp stones biting his palms and knees, tearing at his clothes. Bare rock at the bottom of the slope raced towards him. Tom threw up his arms to shield his face, dipped his shoulder and rolled. He slammed to a stop on his back.

For a moment he lay stunned, staring up at a wide arch of clear blue sky. Then the nagging throb of countless scrapes and bruises brought him back to his senses.

Tom heaved himself over and spotted his sword, just out of reach.

He tried to rise, but a white-hot pain flared in his ankle and he sank back to the ground. He gritted his teeth and reached, pulling his aching body closer to his weapon.

Crunch! Dray's huge boot came down on Tom's outstretched wrist, making him gasp with agony. Tom struggled to free his hand, but the huge man was far too heavy. Dray stooped, lifted Tom's sword

and slowly turned around. Terror
squeezed Tom's chest. His sword
glinted as Dray drew it back ready
to strike. With a flash of victory in
his pale eyes, Dray brought the
blade down.

Thunk! An arrow punched through
Dray's thick forearm. Tom's sword
hit the ground with a clang, while

Dray stared at the hole in his flesh, his bald forehead creased with confusion. Tom twisted his neck and looked back to see Elenna already fitting another arrow to her bow.

Amelia stood at Elenna's side, glaring at Dray, a huge rock between her hands. Tom blinked in confusion.

"GRAAAH!" Amelia charged forwards with a roar and cannoned shoulder-first into Dray, knocking him sideways. Tom, his arm free, scrambled to his knees to see Amelia smash her rock down on Dray's bald head with a sickening crack. Dray crumpled and hit the ground. He lay still, his eyes closed. Tom couldn't see the big hulk breathing, but that

meant nothing. Dray was no mortal –
Tom knew that now.

"Are you all right?" Elenna cried,
as she and Amelia rushed to Tom's
side. Each held out a hand. Tom took
Elenna's, and slowly pulled himself
to his feet. He gasped with pain as he
put weight on his ankle, but it held.
Not broken! Tom thought with relief.
Just a sprain.

"I'm fine," he said. Then he gritted
his teeth, and turned on Amelia.
"I'm not falling for any more of your
tricks!" Tom growled.

Amelia held up her hands. "I'm on
your side now!" she said. "I promise!
I'm not working for Jezrin any more."

Elenna rolled her eyes. "What? Not

now you've been caught, you mean!"

Tom couldn't control his rage. "You should never have been working for him in the first place!" he cried. "You're the descendant of Kara the Fearless – the brave and noble Mistress of the Beasts!"

Amelia looked at her feet. "That's why Jezrin came looking for me," she said, pushing at a stone with her boot. "He told me I was rightful Mistress of the Beasts. He created Dray to be my bodyguard, and gave us a poisoned dart to strike Epos while you were in Gwildor."

Tom shook his head in disgust. "So you could make yourself look like a hero while I looked like a fool?" he said.

Amelia nodded. "The plan was to have you stripped of your title so I could take your place…"

"And when that didn't work, you decided to challenge me for my title instead?" Tom asked.

Amelia kicked the stone away and met Tom's gaze, her cheeks fiery red. "Yes. But now I've worked out that Jezrin was just using me…" She trailed off, and her eyes fell back to the ground.

"There's something more you're not telling me," Tom said.

Amelia tensed. When she finally looked up, her jaw was set, and her blue eyes shone with defiance.

"Jezrin wanted me to kill you," Amelia said. "When you were asleep. But that's a coward's way. I said no!"

Tom suddenly remembered what he'd seen in the jungle, and knew she was telling the truth. "I heard you," he said. "You were arguing with Dray."

Amelia nodded. "Jezrin can talk through Dray. He—"

Elenna gasped and grabbed Tom's sleeve, pointing to the ground where the brute had been lying. "Speaking of Dray," she said, "where is he?"

Read
KARIXA THE DIAMOND WARRIOR
to find out what happens next!

Discover the new Beast Quest mobile game from

Available free on iOS and Android

  **amazon**.com

Guide Tom on his Quest to free the Good Beasts
of Avantia from Malvel's evil spells.

Battle the Beasts, defeat the minions,
unearth the secrets and collect
rewards as you journey through the
Kingdom of Avantia.

DOWNLOAD THE APP TO BEGIN
THE ADVENTURE NOW!